My Weirdtastic School #1

Miss Banks Pulls Lots of Pranks!

Dan Gutman

Pictures by
Jim Paillot

HARPER
An Imprint of HarperCollins*Publishers*

To Sam Brazzini

My Weirdtastic School #1: Miss Banks Pulls Lots of Pranks!
Text copyright © 2023 by Dan Gutman
Illustrations copyright © 2023 by Jim Paillot

Library of Congress Control Number: 2022940750
ISBN 978-0-06-320691-5 (pbk bdg) — ISBN 978-0-06-320692-2 (trade bdg)

Typography by Laura Mock
22 23 24 25 26 LBC 5 4 3 2 1

First Edition

Contents

Bummer after the Summer

My name is A.J., and I know what you're thinking. You're thinking about Oreos. Because that's what I'm thinking about.

Oreos are my favorite cookie. How do they get that yummy cream filling inside each one so perfectly? Do they have machines to do that? Or is some guy sitting in a factory squirting the cream into every single Oreo? Man, that guy must be tired at the end of the day! I wouldn't want to grow up and become an Oreo squirter, that's for sure.

My point is: third grade is finally over and I have to start fourth grade now. Bummer after the summer! In fourth grade, we'll have to learn all new stuff. *Harder* stuff.

Of course, Andrea Young, this annoying girl in my class with curly brown hair, is *soooooooo* excited about moving up to fourth grade. Do you know what the Human Homework Machine did over summer vacation? She didn't hang out with the rest of us kids. She didn't play ball or watch TV or play video games.

No, she studied!

It's true! Andrea needs to be smarter than everybody else in fourth grade. What is her problem?

On the first day of school, I saw Little Miss Know-It-All outside on the steps. She was talking with her crybaby friend, Emily.

"I went to the beach with my family in August," Emily said. "It was so much fun!"

"I taught myself about quadrilaterals and how to do three-digit multiplication," said Andrea.

Quadra-what? I had no idea what she

was talking about. Why can't a truck full of quadrilaterals fall on Andrea's head?

The rest of the gang was coming up the front steps to school.

"Who's gonna be our new teacher?" asked Ryan, who will eat anything, even stuff that isn't food.

"Who's gonna be our new teacher?" asked Michael, who never ties his shoes.

"Who's gonna be our new teacher?" asked Alexia, this girl who rides a skateboard all the time.

In case you were wondering, everybody was asking who would be our new teacher.

We walked a million hundred miles to room 123, which is the fourth-grade classroom. The sign above the door said MISS BANKS.

"Who's Miss Banks?" asked Neil, who we call the nude kid even though he wears clothes. "I never heard of her."

"She must be a new teacher," I said.

That's when the weirdest thing in the history of the world happened. As soon as we stepped on the carpet inside the classroom door, there was a weird popping sound.

POP! POP! POP! POP!

"Eeeeeeek!" screamed Emily.

"Help!" shouted Alexia.

"The aliens have landed!" shouted Ryan.

"Run for your lives!" shouted Neil.

Everybody was yelling and screaming and hooting and hollering and freaking out. Some lady came running over. She picked up the corner of the carpet.

"What's this?" she asked. "Bubble wrap? Hmmm, I wonder who put this bubble wrap under the carpet."

"Who are you?" asked Andrea.

"My name is Miss Banks," the lady told us. "I'll be your teacher this year for fourth grade."

She went over to the whiteboard and wrote MISS BANKS in big letters. Then she told us to take a seat at the desk that had our name on it.

When I sat down, a huge farting noise

came out from under me! Not just from me. Everybody made a huge farting noise when they sat down.

"There's a whoopee cushion on my seat!" yelled Alexia.

"Mine too!" shouted Emily.

"Hmmm," said Miss Banks. "I wonder who put those there. Anyway, we're going to have a wonderful year together. Does anybody have a question about fourth grade?"

Andrea was waving her hand in the air like she was trying to signal a plane from a desert island. But I raised my hand, and Miss Banks called on me first. So nah-nah-nah boo-boo on Andrea.

PPPFFT!!!

"How old are you?" I asked Miss Banks.

"That's not nice, Arlo!" said Andrea, who calls me by my real name because she knows I don't like it. "You're not supposed to ask grown-ups how old they are."

Why not? Who made that dumb rule?

"Oh, I don't mind you asking my age," said Miss Banks. "I'm one hundred and forty-two years old."

"WOW," everybody said, which is "MOM" upside down.

"You don't look that old," said Ryan.

"Well, I use a very good moisturizer," replied Miss Banks.

"I have a question," said Neil. "Why are you wearing two different-colored socks?"

Neil was right. Miss Banks had a red sock on her left foot and a blue sock on her right foot.

"Oh," she said. "I have another pair of socks just like this one at home."

WHAT?!

"Well," continued Miss Banks, "if both of your socks are the same color, how can you tell you have them on the right feet?"*

I looked down at my socks. Maybe they were on the wrong feet. I didn't even know that we were supposed to wear certain socks on certain feet. Fourth grade had just started, and I already learned something!

---

*Hmm, good point.

Andrea was still waving her hand in the air like she was washing a really big window, so Miss Banks called on her.

"I brought you a present, Miss Banks," Andrea said sweetly.

Of course! I knew Andrea wouldn't waste any time sucking up to the new teacher. She went over to Miss Banks's desk and put an apple on it.

"Why, thank you, Andrea!"

Miss Banks took a bite of the apple. Then she stopped for a moment, looked frightened, and grabbed her throat with both hands.

"Allergic . . . to . . . apples . . ." she groaned. "Need . . . water . . . going . . . to die!"

Then she fell on the floor.

We all rushed out into the hall to get water from the water fountain for Miss Banks. But when we got back to class, she was standing there like nothing unusual had happened.

"Just kidding!" she said. "I'm not allergic to apples."

"Hey," Ryan whispered to me, "the new

teacher is cool!"

Andrea raised her hand again.

"What are we going to learn in fourth grade, Miss Banks?" she asked.

"Well," Miss Banks replied, "today I'm going to give you a little sneak peek at what we'll be studying in math, social studies, science, and your other subjects. Doesn't that sound like fun?"

"Yes!" shouted all the girls.

"No!" shouted all the boys.

"But first"—Miss Banks went over and picked up a big plate from her desk—"who wants a brownie?"

"I do!"

"I do!"

"I do!"

In case you were wondering, everybody wanted a brownie. Of course! Brownies are almost as good as Oreos. I could eat a brownie for breakfast, lunch, and dinner. It's the perfect food.

"Do you have any Oreos?" I asked.

"No, just brownies," replied Miss Banks.

She took the plastic wrap off the plate, came over to my desk, and said I could pick any brownie I wanted.

There was just one problem. There weren't any brownies on the plate! It was filled with a bunch of letter *E*s cut out of brown-colored paper.

"Those aren't brownies!" I shouted.

"Sure they are," said Miss Banks, holding one up for everybody to see. "They're brown *Es*! Aha-ha! Get it? Brownies? Brown *Es*?"

Miss Banks is weird.

Spelling Can Be Tricky

2

"Okay, let's start with spelling," Miss Banks announced after we pledged the allegiance. "You kids are going to become great spellers in fourth grade."

"I love spelling!" said Andrea, who loves anything to do with school.

"Me too!" said Emily, who loves everything Andrea loves.

"That's great," said Miss Banks, "because spelling is very important. If you want to get ahead in the world, you need to know how to spell. But spelling can also be tricky. For instance, who can spell the word 'spell'?"

"Oooooh . . . oooooh . . . ooooh!"

Andrea looked like she was going to pop a lung if Miss Banks didn't call on her.

"'Spell' is spelled S-P-E-L-L," Andrea said proudly.

As if that was hard! Any dumbhead knows how to spell the word "spell."

"Very good, Andrea," said Miss Banks. "Now, can you spell the word 'misspell'?"

"M-I-S-P-E-L-L," said Andrea.

"No, sorry," said Miss Banks. "There are

two *s*'s in 'misspell.' You spelled 'spell' correctly, but you misspelled 'misspell.' See what I mean about spelling being tricky?"

Andrea looked mad, like it was Miss Banks's fault that she misspelled "misspell." It may have been the first time in her life that Little Miss Perfect made a mistake.

"Let's try another one," said Miss Banks. "Who can spell the word 'wrong'? A.J., how about you?"

"Sure," I said. "I can spell any word wrong."

Everybody laughed even though I didn't say anything funny.

"Go ahead, A.J.," said Miss Banks. "Spell it."

"I-T," I said. "It."

"No," said Miss Banks. "Spell the word 'wrong.'"

"What word?" I asked.

"'Wrong,'" said Miss Banks.

"How can I be wrong?" I complained. "I didn't even spell the word yet!"

"I mean spell the word 'wrong,' A.J.," said Miss Banks. "Like when you do something wrong."

"Oh," I said. "That's different. R-O-N-G."

"I'm sorry," said Miss Banks. "That's wrong."

"But you told me to spell the word 'wrong'!" I complained.

"I mean you spelled 'wrong' wrong," said Miss Banks.

"I can spell 'wrong'!" shouted Andrea. "'Wrong' is spelled W-R-O-N-G."

"That's right, Andrea," said Miss Banks.

"No," I said. "'Right' is R-I-G-H-T. Andrea's wrong."

"Well, you spelled 'right' right, A.J.," said Miss Banks. "But you spelled 'wrong' wrong. Andrea spelled 'wrong' right, and—"

Miss Banks stopped for a moment, took a handkerchief out of her pocket, and wiped her forehead with it.

"Okay, I'm going to pass out—"

"She's gonna pass out!" Michael shouted. "Call an ambulance!"

"Give her air!" shouted Alexia.

"I'm going to pass out sheets of paper," continued Miss Banks.

Ohhhhhhhh. They should definitely have different ways to say "pass out."

"We're going to have a little spelling test," said Miss Banks, "to see how well you spell."

Ugh. I hate tests. We all took out pencils as Miss Banks passed around the papers.

"I'm going to say ten words," said Miss Banks. "You try to spell them. Ready?"

It seemed simple enough.

"Is there a prize for the winner?" asked Andrea, who loves winning prizes. She probably has a trophy room at home with all the prizes she's won.

"No," said Miss Banks. "This is just for fun. Your first word is . . . 'burf.'"

What?

"What's a burf?" whispered Neil.

I never heard of a burf. But teachers always tell us that if we can't spell a word, we should try to sound it out. I wrote

B-U-R-F on my paper.

"The next word is 'spinkheimer,'" said Miss Banks.

That's a tough one. I tried to sound it out. It wasn't easy.

"The next word is 'splurgle.'"

"Can you use that in a sentence?" asked Alexia.

"Sure," said Miss Banks. "Please splurgle the dungle before it runs out of plark."

What?

She asked us to spell a bunch of other words. Boonch. Carpendoodle. Felgenburger. I never heard of any of those words.

"Wait a minute," said Alexia. "You made those words up!"

"Don't be silly," said Miss Banks. "I've learned a lot of words in my one hundred and forty-two years."

"This spelling test is really hard," Andrea complained.

Andrea was probably afraid she was going to fail a test for the first time in her life. Then she won't get into Harvard.

At the end, we passed our papers forward. Miss Banks collected them. Then she did the weirdest thing in the history of the world. She ripped our spelling tests in half and threw them in the garbage can.

WHAT?!

"Aren't you going to grade our spelling tests?" asked Emily.

"Why should I?" Miss Banks replied.

"None of those words are real. I made them all up. Let's move on. Can anybody spell the words 'race car' backward?"

"Oooooh, I can!" shouted Little Miss Know-It-All. "'Race car' backward is R-A-C-E C-A-R. It's a palindrome, which is a word or phrase that's spelled the same way backward and forward."

Andrea smiled the smile she smiles to let everybody know she knows something nobody else knows.

"Very good, Andrea!" said Miss Banks. "And can you spell 'race car' upside down?"

Huh? Andrea looked puzzled. We all did.

Miss Banks got down on the floor. Then she stood on her head.

"R-A-C-E C-A-R," she said. "That's 'race car,' upside down."

Then she got back on her feet again.

"Do you kids know what a word search is?" she asked.

Of course I know what a word search is. It's when you have a bunch of letters on a page and you have to find the words that are hidden in the letters.

Miss Banks passed out another sheet of paper for each of us.

"There are ten words hidden in this grid," she told us. "See if you can find them."

Andrea grabbed her paper and got to work. I could see that she was excited. She loves to be first at stuff, because that means she can feel like she's better than everybody else.

"I'll be back in a minute," said Miss Banks, and she left the class. I looked at the sheet . . .

That word search was hard!

"Did you find any words yet?" Ryan whispered to me.

A I B J C K D L E M F N G O H
N A H N A H N A H B O O B O O
P Q R S U T V I W X Y Z A A Z
L M T N T O U P V Q W R X S E
I O H N G M F P E L D K C J B
A I B J C K D L E L F M G N H
O P U Q O R W S I T Y Q E R A
S F F E Q D K C M B X A C D X
B H C I D J E K F L G M Z N W
O W P X Q Y R Z S N T A U E V
I A H B I C J D K E C U C F L
V F B M C B D D I F J H K R L
M V N U O W P X Q Z R Y S Q T
A C M A F D M R E C B N E D B
S T R X L B K I R B L Y B Z A

"No," I said. "I don't see any."

"Me neither," said Andrea.

WOW. If Miss Know-It-All can't find the words, nobody can.

"Is nah-nah-nah boo-boo a word?" asked Alexia.

"I don't think so," replied Neil.

Miss Banks came back into the class.

"So how are you kids making out?" she asked.

"We're not making out!" I shouted. "We're doing a word search. And we can't find the words."

"I looked all over the grid," said Michael. "The only thing that even looks like a word is nah-nah-nah boo-boo."

"You're right," replied Miss Banks. "So nah-nah-nah boo-boo on you!"

"Huh?" said Emily. "Why did you give this to us?"

"Well," said Miss Banks, "I said it was a word search. I didn't say it was a word find. I think you learned a valuable life lesson here. You can search forever, but sometimes you won't find what you're looking for."

That's when the weirdest thing in the history of the world happened. I looked out the window and saw that it was snowing outside. That was weird. It was September.

Miss Banks's cell phone rang.

"Excuse me," she told us, "I need to take this important call. It's from Mrs. Stoker, the principal."

Miss Banks listened for a minute, and then she said into the phone, "Okay, so we're leaving at ten o'clock?"

WHAT?! I looked at the clock. It was a few minutes before ten. Yes! Snow day!

This was the greatest day of my life. Everybody was hooting and hollering.

"*WOOOO-HOOO!*"

We all rushed to get our coats and backpacks from our cubbies.

"What are you kids doing?" asked Miss Banks.

"We're getting ready to go home," I told her.

"Why?" asked Miss Banks. "It's not dismissal time. The day just started."

"But . . . we heard you on the phone with Mrs. Stoker," said Ryan. "You said—"

"April Fools!" shouted Miss Banks.

WHAT?!

"It's not April!" shouted Neil.

"Every day is April Fools' Day to me!" said Miss Banks.

Man, Miss Banks pulls lots of pranks!*

---

*Hey, that's a good idea for a book title!

Pop Quiz

"Time for a pop quiz!" announced Miss Banks.

Ugh. I hate pop quizzes. Do they have pop quizzes at your school? If they don't, you're lucky. A pop quiz is when your teacher gives you a test for no reason, and with no warning. You can't study for it. You don't know what's going to be on it.

The teacher can ask you anything.

Miss Banks told us to take out a pencil as she passed around a sheet of paper to each of us.

"This will be easy," she told us. "The instructions are simple. There are ten questions. Read the quiz all the way through before answering the first question. Go!"

I looked at the sheet. The first question said . . .

1. What's your name? Write it at the top of this sheet.

I wrote my name at the top of the sheet and moved on to . . .

2. Add up these numbers: 8 + 4 + 10 + 15 + 99 = ?

It was too hard to do the math in my head.

"Can we use scrap paper?" I asked Miss Banks.

"If you feel you need to," she replied.

I took out a piece of scrap paper and started writing the numbers down. Then I added them up. It came to 136. I wrote that down.

I looked around. Everybody was working on the math problem. Well, everybody except Andrea. She was just sitting there with her hands folded, like she was finished already. How could she be done so quickly? I better work faster. I moved on to . . .

3. Circle every T *on this page.*

I circled every *T* on the page. That was easy. I moved on to number four . . .

4. *What time is it when the big hand is on four and the little hand is on eleven?*

I drew a clock on my scrap paper and put in the hands. It was twenty minutes after eleven. I wrote that down and peeked around to see how everybody else was doing. Emily and Alexia were sitting there with their hands folded. Man, girls work fast! I moved on to . . .

5. *Silently recite the first six words of the Gettysburg Address.*

Oh, I knew that one: "Four score and seven years ago." I moved on to . . .

6. *Get up, walk around your desk in a circle, and then sit down.*

That's a weird thing to ask on a pop quiz. But what do I know? Maybe things are different in fourth grade. I got up, walked around my desk, and sat down. So did Ryan, Michael, and Neil. I moved on to . . .

7. Write your name backward.

I wrote my name backward. Then I moved on to . . .

8. Stand up and sing a line from "Old MacDonald Had a Farm."

I got up and sang, "Old MacDonald had a farm, E-I-E-I-O."

Michael got up and sang, "Old Mac-Donald had a farm, E-I-E-I-O."

I looked around. Ryan and Neil were sitting there with their hands folded. How

come they didn't get up and sing? Maybe
they did it and I didn't notice. I moved on
to . . .

*9. Cluck like a chicken while standing
on one foot.*

"Bok! Bok! Bok!" I said, standing on one
foot.

I looked around. Nobody else was standing on one foot. Nobody else was clucking.

"Hey, you guys! Why aren't you doing it?" I asked.

They didn't answer. Then I looked at the last question on the bottom of the page . . .

10. Do not answer any of the questions or complete any of the tasks on this pop quiz. Put down your pencil and sit with your hands folded. Don't say anything to anybody.

WHAT?!

I looked at Andrea. She was sitting there with her hands folded and a big smile on her face.

Ryan had his hands folded. Alexia had her hands folded. Michael had his hands folded. Emily had her hands folded. Neil had his hands folded. Everybody except me was sitting there with their hands folded.

Then they all started cracking up, even Miss Banks.

"Hey, what's going on?" I asked.

"It was a fake pop quiz, dumbhead!" Andrea said. "Miss Banks told us to read the quiz all the way through before answering any questions. She just wanted to see if we knew how to follow instructions!"

"That's right!" said Miss Banks.

I wanted to say something mean to

Andrea, but I couldn't come up with anything good.

"Your *face* needs to follow instructions!" I shouted at her.

Suddenly, the door opened and our principal, Mrs. Stoker, came into the classroom. Everybody stopped laughing.

"Good morning!" she said cheerfully. "May I tell you a joke?"

"Sure!" everybody shouted.

"This boy comes home after the first day of school," said Mrs. Stoker, "and his mom asks him what he learned. He says, 'Not enough. I have to go back tomorrow.'"

Everybody laughed even though the joke wasn't all that funny. Mrs. Stoker is the principal, so you have to laugh at her jokes. That's the law.

"I just wanted to see how you kids were doing on your first day of fourth grade," said Mrs. Stoker.

"We're doing terrible!" I said.

"What's the matter?" she asked.

"Miss Banks gave us a fake pop quiz," said Andrea, giggling, "and A.J. totally fell for it."

"Yeah, he was singing 'Old MacDonald Had a Farm,'" said Alexia.

"And he was clucking like a chicken," added Neil.

Everybody started laughing at me again. It's not fair! I wanted to run away to Antarctica and go live with the penguins. Penguins don't have to take dumb spelling tests or fake pop quizzes or do phony word searches. Penguins don't pull pranks on each other either.*

---

*Enjoying the book so far? Can we get you a pillow so you'll be more comfortable?

Hunting the Sloof Lirpa

"Before we move on to science," announced Miss Banks, "who wants a doughnut?"

"I do!"

"I do!"

"I do!"

In case you were wondering, everybody wanted a doughnut. I love doughnuts.

They're my second-favorite treat, right after Oreos.

"Do you have any Oreos?" I asked.

"No," said Miss Banks. "Just doughnuts."

She brought out a big box and said each of us could take one doughnut. Neil went first.

"Wait a minute!" Neil shouted after he looked inside the box. "Those aren't dough-nuts! They're carrots and cucumbers and broccoli and a bunch of other veggies!"

"WHAT?!" yelled Miss Banks. "This is an outrage! I asked for doughnuts. How did those veggies get in here? I want my money back!"

Ugh, veggies. I can't believe grown-ups expect us to eat stuff that grew out of the dirt. The only person who ate the veggies was Ryan. Of course, he'll eat *anything*.

"What are we going to learn in science this year?" asked Andrea, who only wants to learn stuff so she can show off how smart she is.

"Oh, we're going to learn about the planets and space and stars and electricity and the water cycle and weather and *blah blah blah blah* . . ."

Miss Banks went on for like a million hundred years. What a snoozefest.

"But today, we're going out for a science field trip," she said. "We're going birding."*

Miss Banks grabbed some binoculars

---

*Birding is when you look at birds, so it has the perfect name.

from her desk drawer. We all lined up and went out to the playground. At the edge of the playground are some woods.

"Shhhhh!" whispered Miss Banks as she tiptoed into the woods. "We're going to hunt for the elusive Sloof Lirpa."

I never heard of a bird called Sloof Lirpa. It must be some really exotic bird. Miss Banks told us the Sloof Lirpa was red and yellow, and it had been spotted in the area. But it's very rare. She passed out binoculars for all of us.

I looked around, but I didn't see any birds at all, much less a Sloof Lirpa. Miss Banks told us how the Sloof Lirpa flies, what it eats, how it raises its young, and other stuff. She opened a bag of marshmallows and gave one to each of us.

"The Sloof Lirpa has been known to swoop down and take a marshmallow right out of your hand," said Miss Banks. "It's the most glorious thing!"

"Ooooh, I hope we'll see one," Emily said as we tiptoed through the woods.

"Sloof Lirpa!" hollered Miss Banks, holding a marshmallow over her head. "Sloof Lirpa! Loof-aloof-*aloooooo*!"

"What's that?" Ryan asked.

"That's the Sloof Lirpa mating call," replied Miss Banks. "You try it."

"Sloof Lirpa! Sloof Lirpa!" we all called, "Loof-aloof-*alooooo*!"

"Flap your arms like a bird," instructed Miss Banks. "That attracts them."

We all flapped our arms and called out, "Sloof Lirpa! Sloof Lirpa! Loof-aloof-*alooooo*!" There were some birds flying around, but I didn't see a Sloof Lirpa.

"Maybe the Sloof Lirpas are hibernating," suggested Alexia. "Like bears."

"We just need to keep looking," said Miss Banks. "I know they're out here somewhere."

We tiptoed around for a million hundred hours. Not a Sloof Lirpa in sight.

Suddenly, Andrea stopped in her tracks.

"Wait a minute!" she said.

"Did you see one?" I asked. "Did you see a Sloof Lirpa?"

"No," Andrea replied. "We're not going to see any Sloof Lirpas out here."

"Why not?" asked Emily.

"Because there's no such thing as a Sloof Lirpa!" said Andrea.

"How do you know?" asked Michael.

"I just figured it out," Andrea told us.
"SLOOF LIRPA is APRIL FOOLS backward!"
WHAT?!

Loof-aloof-aloooooo!

Smell-O-Vision

Miss Banks laughed her head off after she tricked the whole class into walking around the woods, flapping our arms, and calling out "Sloof Lirpa" over and over again. She even shot a video of us on her cell phone. I bet she's going to show it to the teachers in the teachers' lounge.

Miss Daisy, our second-grade teacher, was weird. Mr. Granite and Mr. Cooper, our third-grade teachers, were weird too. But now that I'm older and wiser and in fourth grade, I'm beginning to think Miss Banks is the weirdest teacher of *all* of them.

"Before we move on to math," she announced, "who wants gum?"

"I do!"

"I do!"

"I do!"

In case you were wondering, everybody said they wanted gum.

To be honest, I'm not a big gum fan. Gum is okay, but it loses its flavor and tastes yucky after five minutes. Then you have to keep this tasteless ball of gunk in your mouth until you can find a garbage can.

But I said "I do" anyway when Miss Banks offered us gum. Why? Because teachers never give us gum! They're always telling us to spit *out* our gum.

"Do you have any Oreos?" I asked. "I'm not a big gum fan."

"No," said Miss Banks. "I just have gum."

She brought around a plate with a bunch of pieces of gum on it, and they were all different colors. I picked a green piece and popped it in my mouth.

Yuck! It tasted *awful.*

"This isn't gum!" shouted Ryan. "It's Play-Doh!"*

"Ugh! Gross," I shouted. "It's terrible!"

---

*Kids, don't try this at home! Don't eat Play-Doh!

"Oops!" said Miss Banks. "My mistake! Aha-ha! Time is fun when you're having flies!"

What did that mean? I can't believe I fell for another one of Miss Banks's pranks! I should have known better and refused to eat the gum.

That's it. I promised myself that I would

never ever eat anything else that Miss Banks offered me.

"What are we going to learn in math this year?" asked Miss I-Want-to-Know-Everything.

"Oh, we're going to learn about per-centages and fractions and decimals and three-digit multiplication and *blah blah blah blah . . ."*

Zzzzzzzzzzz. Oh, sorry. I dozed off there for a minute. It's hard to keep my eyes open when anyone is talking about math.

"But today I have a special surprise for you," said Miss Banks.

Uh-oh. I could only imagine what kind of surprise she was going to pull on us. I was expecting the worst. But Miss Banks opened a big box and pulled out a bunch of laptop computers. She handed one to each of us.

"These are called Domebooks," she told us. "All fourth graders in the district get them."

"Are they free?" asked Emily.

"Yes," said Miss Banks. "Just take good care of your Domebook and give it back at the end of the school year."

Cool! I always wanted my own laptop so I could play video games on school time.

"These laptops are not for playing video games on school time," Miss Banks warned us. "We're going to use them for lots of subjects, including math. In fourth grade, you're going to learn about mixed numbers and *blah blah blah blah . . ."*

She went on like that for a million hundred hours. I thought I was gonna die from old age. Finally, she told us how to turn on our Domebooks.

"These are very advanced laptops," Miss Banks explained. "They have a built-in app that produces smells to go with certain numbers. Like when you press the number one key, the screen gives off a smell like an apple. And when you press the number two key, it smells like strawberry. It's called Smell-O-Vision, and it's going to help you learn math."

I never heard of laptops giving off smells. But I guess it could be possible. They're doing amazing things with computers these days.

"Go ahead," said Miss Banks. "Try it."

We all started pressing the keys on our Domebooks to see what smells came out.

"I think I smell it!" said Andrea. "It's . . . cinnamon!"

"Me too!" said Emily, who smells everything that Andrea smells.

"The number three key smells like roses!" said Neil.

"The number eight key smells like a hamburger!" said Michael.

I pressed all the keys on my keyboard

and sniffed the screen. It just smelled like a computer to me.

"I can't smell anything," I said.

"Put your nose right up close to the screen, A.J.," said Miss Banks.

"Maybe you have a bad sense of smell, Arlo," said Andrea.

"Your *face* has a bad sense of smell!" I told her.

But maybe Andrea was right. Maybe I don't smell very good. Wait, let me put that in different words. Maybe I can't smell stuff very well.

I put my nose close to the screen and sniffed for a long time, trying to catch a whiff of something. And you'll never believe who poked her head into the door at that moment.

Nobody! Why would you poke your head into a door? That would hurt. But you'll never believe who poked her head into the door*way*.

It was the Ella Mentry School computer teacher, Mrs. Yonkers!

"I hope you're enjoying your Domebooks," she said. "They're going to come in handy this year. Uh, why is A.J. sniffing his screen?"

"Beats me," said Miss Banks. "Kids do weird things."

"But . . . but . . . but . . ." I said. "You told us . . ."

Miss Banks laughed because I said "but," which sounds just like "butt" even though it only has one *T*.

Won't Get Fooled Again

That's it! I'm not going to fall for any more of Miss Banks's pranks. There's an old saying that goes, "Fool me once, shame on me. Fool me twice . . ." Uh, well, I don't remember the rest. It goes something like that.*

---

*You can look it up for yourself.

"Before we move on to social studies," said Miss Banks, "who wants a cookie?"

"Not me!" I shouted.

"I don't," said Andrea.

"Me neither," said Emily.

In case you were wondering, nobody wanted one of Miss Banks's cookies.

"What?" said Miss Banks. "I thought kids *love* cookies. What's wrong with you?"

"You're just going to pull another one of your pranks on us," said Alexia.

"Who? Me?" asked Miss Banks, like she was surprised. "Pranks? I have no idea what you're talking about!"

"You offered us brownies that weren't

brownies," said Michael. "Then you offered us doughnuts that weren't doughnuts. Then you offered us gum that wasn't gum. So I bet your cookies aren't really cookies either."

"That's right," we all said.

Miss Banks looked hurt. She took a box out of her desk drawer.

"Suit yourselves," she said as she sat down and put her feet up on her desk. "More cookies for me."

She reached into the box and took out a cookie. It looked a lot like . . .

NOOOOOOOOOOOOOOO!

"Is that . . . an Oreo?" I asked.

"Of course," said Miss Banks. "I love

Oreos. They're my favorite kind of cookie."

Mine too! She took a bite of the Oreo and then closed her eyes as she chewed it really slowly. Then she took another bite.

It looked like she was chewing the Oreo in slow motion.

"Mmmmmmm," she moaned. "You kids don't know what you're missing."

I was drooling. That Oreo looked *soooooo* good. It looked like one of those double-stuffed Oreos too. They have twice as much stuffing, so they have the perfect name. I wanted an Oreo more than anything in the history of the world.

"Yum!" Miss Banks said as she finished her Oreo.

Maybe for once, she wasn't pranking us.

"Okay, okay!" I finally shouted. "Can I have an Oreo?"

"Me too!" said Ryan.

"Me three!" said Michael.

"Me four!" said Alexia.

"That's the spirit!" Miss Banks said. She took her feet off her desk and gave each of us an Oreo.

Cookies in school! This was the greatest day of my life!

I took a bite out of the Oreo.

It took about two seconds for me to realize that it tasted funny. The Oreo didn't taste like an Oreo.

"Ugh! Gross! Disgusting!" I said.

"What is this?" asked Alexia.

"Oh, I forgot to mention something," said Miss Banks. "I filled the Oreos with toothpaste."

WHAT?!

"Haven't you heard?" said Miss Banks. "This is the latest thing in dental hygiene. With toothpaste-flavored Oreos, kids can eat cookies and fight cavities at the same time! Aha-ha! Time is fun when you're having flies!"

Antisocial Studies

We were all really mad that Miss Banks gave us toothpaste-filled Oreos. Nobody took another bite. Well, nobody except Ryan, of course. He'll eat anything.

"Miss Banks," said Little Miss Perfect, "what are we going to learn in social studies this year?"

"Oh, we're going to learn about the thirteen colonies and Lewis and Clark and geography and the Revolutionary War and the Bill of Rights* and the three branches of government and *blah blah blah blah . . .*"

Zzzzzzzzzzzzzzzzzzzzzzzz . . .

Oh, sorry. I dozed off again.

Brrrrrriiiiinnnnnnggggg!

It was the lunch bell. That woke me up. Our lunch bell makes a sound like the word "bring." Nobody knows why. Everybody started lining up to go to the vomitorium.

---

*If we have the Bill of Rights, we should have the Rights of Guys Named Bill.

"A.J.," said Miss Banks, "before you go to lunch, may I speak with you for a moment?"

"OOOOOOH!" everybody oooooohed. "A.J.'s in trouble!"

When everybody had left the room, Miss Banks came over to my desk.

"I just wanted you to know," she told me, "that I'm not picking on you. I like to pull pranks on all of my students. It's what I do."

"That's okay," I told her. "I can handle it."

"Great!" she said as she went over to the sink and filled two glasses with water. "I bet you can't balance a glass of water on both hands at the same time."

Hey, nobody tells *me* what I can or can't do.

"I bet I can," I told her.

"Here," Miss Banks said, "put your hands on your desk, palms down."

I put my hands on my desk. Miss Banks carefully put one of the glasses of water on my left hand. Then she put the other glass of water on my right hand.

"See?" I said. "I can balance both of them at the same time."

"I guess you're right," she said. "Very good, A.J. I'll see you later."

And then she walked out of the room.

"But—"

I looked around. I was all by myself in the classroom. I had two glasses of water on my hands. If I moved either of my hands even a little bit, the glasses would fall off and water would spill all over my desk and stuff! There was nothing I could do!

"Miss Banks!" I shouted.

But she was gone. She had pranked me! Again!

"Help!" I shouted. "Somebody! Help!"

I was standing there with the glasses of water on my hands for like a million hundred hours! It looked like I was going to be there for the rest of my life! To make things worse, I suddenly realized that I had to go to the bathroom. I didn't know what to do!

And you'll never believe who walked into the door at that moment.

Nobody! Why would you walk into a door? You could break your nose! I thought we went over this in Chapter

Five. But you'll never believe who walked into the door*way.*

It was Mrs. Stoker, our principal!

"A.J.," she said. "Why aren't you at lunch with the rest of your class?"

"Miss Banks pranked me!" I said. "She bet I couldn't balance these glasses of

water on my hands. Then she left me like this. And now I have to go to the bathroom!"

I was trying not to cry.

"Calm down, A.J.," Mrs. Stoker said as she picked up the glasses. "You can go to the bathroom and then meet your class in the lunchroom."

I walked a million hundred miles to the bathroom. After I did my business, I washed my hands and went over to the paper towel dispenser to dry them off.

There was a sticker on the front of the paper towel dispenser that said "Voice Activated." Hmmmm, that was new. They must have installed voice-activated paper towel dispensers over the summer.

"Give me a paper towel," I said to the paper towel dispenser.

No paper towel came out.

I guess you have to say "please."

"Please give me a paper towel," I said to the paper towel dispenser.

No paper towel came out.

I was getting a little mad.

"I WANT a paper towel," I said a little louder to the paper towel dispenser.

No paper towel came out.

I tapped the paper towel dispenser on the top. Maybe that would shake some paper towels loose.

No paper towel came out.

"GIVE ME A PAPER TOWEL!" I shouted. "NOW!"

No paper towel came out.

I was *really* mad. I banged my fist on the paper towel dispenser, over and over again. But no paper towel came out. I was sweating. And you'll never believe who walked into the door at that moment.

Nobody! Are you kidding me? We went over this just a few paragraphs ago! People don't walk into doors! But you'll never believe who opened the door at that moment.

It was Mr. Macky, the Ella Mentry School reading specialist!

"Are you okay, A.J.?" he asked. "Did I

just hear you yelling at somebody? You're all alone in here."

"I'm trying to get a paper towel!" I shouted.

Mr. Macky looked at the paper towel dispenser.

"Did you push the button?" he asked.

"No," I replied.

He pushed the button. A paper towel slid out.

"But I thought—"

"The paper towel dispenser isn't voice activated," Mr. Macky told me. "Somebody must have put this label on it as a prank."

"Miss Banks!" I shouted. "It *had* to be Miss Banks! This means war!"

This Means War!

Smoke was pouring out of my ears.

Well, not really. But if smoke could pour out of somebody's ears, it definitely would have been pouring out of mine.

I walked a million hundred miles to the vomitorium for lunch. It used to be called the cafetorium, but then some first grader threw up in there. I saw all my friends sitting at our usual table. Our lunch lady, Ms. Hall, was behind the counter.

"We have a special lunch today," she told me. "You have the choice of frog legs, fish eyeballs, roasted grasshoppers, or braunschweiger."

"What's braunschweiger?" I asked.

"It's a sausage that tastes like what a wet dog smells like," said Ms. Hall.

Ugh. I thought I was gonna throw up.

"I'm not hungry," I said.

"Just kidding!" said Ms. Hall. "Do you want a hot dog, a grilled cheese sandwich, or chicken strips?"

Now the *other* grown-ups were pulling

pranks on me! It was contagious!

I took a hot dog and went over to the table where everybody was sitting. I told the gang what Miss Banks did to me with the glasses of water and the voice-activated paper towel dispenser.

"She's out to get me," I complained as I took a bite out of my hot dog.

"She's out to get *all* of us," Michael said.

"Miss Banks pulls lots of pranks," said Neil. "She's like a prank machine."

"We've got to get back at her," I said, lowering my voice so they couldn't hear me at the other tables.

"Yeah," everybody agreed, even Andrea and Emily.

"We're not gonna take it," whispered Neil. "If Miss Banks is going to prank us all the time, we should prank her right back!"

"Yeah," whispered Ryan. "We'll show *her*!"

"Nobody pranks us and gets away with it," whispered Alexia.

"That's right!" I whispered.

"So what can we do to get back at her?" asked Andrea.

Hmmm. For once in her life, Andrea had a good question. None of us had ever pranked a teacher before. This was new territory.

"We could get some fake vomit and put it on her chair," Michael suggested.

"Nah," I said. "That's the oldest trick in the book."

"Where would we get fake vomit anyway?" asked Ryan.

"From Rent-Fake-Vomit," I said. "You can rent anything."

"We could put yellow sticky notes all over her car," suggested Neil. "That would be funny."

"I don't know if Miss Banks has a car," I said.

"What if we TP'd her house?" suggested Michael.

"We don't know where she lives," said Ryan.

"We could put soy sauce in her coffee," suggested Alexia. "That would be nasty."

"We could empty out her desk drawer and fill it with Cheerios," suggested Emily.

"We don't have any soy sauce or Cheerios," I reminded them.

"Then what are we gonna do?" asked Neil.

I thought about it. Then I thought about it some more. I thought so hard that I thought my head was going to explode.

I looked at the clock. Soon it would be time for dismissal. We had to come up with something fast. Emily got up to scrape her tray into the garbage can. As she did, one of her books fell off the table.

That's when I came up with the most brilliant idea for a prank in the history of pranks. We put our heads together like a football team in a huddle, and I whispered my great idea to everybody.

"That's genius!" said Ryan. "You should get the Nobel Prize for that one, A.J."*

You probably want to know what my genius idea was. You're probably *dying* to know.

Well, I'm not gonna tell you.

Okay, okay, I'll tell you. But you have to read the next chapter. So nah-nah-nah boo-boo on you!

But I will tell you something right now. This was going to be the greatest prank in the history of pranks.

---

*That's a prize they give out to people who don't have bells.

The Prank of the Century

We walked a million hundred miles to room 123. I couldn't wait to pull off the prank of the century. I was rubbing my hands together with excitement. That's what you do when you're excited. You rub your hands together. Nobody knows why.

When we walked into the room, Miss

Banks was waiting for us.

"For homework tonight," she said, "please read the first five chapters in your social studies book, write an essay on what you did over summer vacation, and create a life-size animal out of items you have around the house."

WHAT?!

"Just kidding!" said Miss Banks. "There's no homework tonight. But starting tomorrow, we're going to work on multidigit multiplication, the parts of speech, and *blah blah blah blah . . ."*

That fake homework assignment was just another one of Miss Banks's pranks, of course. Well, she had her little fun. But now it was *my* turn. It was time to begin my counterattack. While Miss Banks was talking, I put my hand in the air.

"Do you have a question, A.J.?" she asked.

"No," I told her. "I'm just pointing at the ceiling."

A few kids giggled.

But that wasn't my genius prank. No,

I was going to start off easy. I wanted to warm up before I unleashed my genius prank to end all pranks.

"Very funny, A.J.," said Miss Banks. "As I was saying, starting tomorrow, we're going to work on adding and subtracting fractions and *blah blah blah blah . . .*"

She passed out a handout. After I got mine, I put my hand up in the air again.

"Yes, A.J.?" Miss Banks asked.

"I don't get it," I said.

"What don't you get, A.J.?"

"I don't understand how they can take a tree and turn it into this thin sheet of paper," I said.

A few kids giggled. Miss Banks stopped passing out her handout and looked at me for a moment. She seemed a little annoyed. Good.

"Neither do I, A.J.," muttered Miss Banks. "Now back to our work for tomorrow. We're going to learn about the solar system, electricity, and *blah blah blah blah . . .*"

I could see I was getting to her. I looked at the clock on the wall. It was four minutes before two o'clock. Perfect. It was time for me to move in for the kill. It was time to give Miss Banks a taste of her own medicine.*

Here's the awesome prank I told the gang about during lunch: At exactly two o'clock, everybody in the class was going

---

*Huh? Who else would taste your medicine?

to drop our books on the floor. All at the same time. It would be hilarious. Even Andrea and Emily agreed to do it. This was going to be great!

"Blah blah blah blah..." said Miss Banks.

As she spoke, we were all peeking at the clock. It was three minutes before two o'clock. I piled my books up on top of my desk.

"Blah blah blah blah..." said Miss Banks.

It was two minutes before two o'clock. I looked over at Ryan, and he looked over at me. It was hard not to laugh, thinking about the great prank we were about to pull off.

It was one minute before two o'clock. This was going to be awesome.

We all watched the clock as the second hand moved closer to the twelve. Alexia gave me a quick thumbs-up, and I gave her one back.

10 ... 9 ... 8 ... 7 ... 6 ... 5 ... 4 ...

Tick, tick, tick.

It was time! As the second hand reached the twelve, I swept my arm across my desk. My books went flying. *Everybody's* books went flying.

BAM! All the books hit the floor.

"AHHHHHHH!" Miss Banks swung around and screamed. The noise took her by surprise. I thought she was going to jump out of her skin.

"Okay, I've had it with you kids!" she shouted. "That's the last straw!"

Huh? What did straws have to do with anything?

Miss Banks looked really mad! I thought she was going to put us in detention for the rest of our lives. But she didn't.

"I quit!" she shouted. And then she walked out of the room, slamming the door behind her.

WOW. That's "MOM" upside down.

It was so quiet in room 123, you could have heard a pin drop. That is, if anybody brought a pin to school with them. But who brings pins to school?

Then everybody started cheering.

"We did it!" said Ryan, giving me a high five. "We pranked her good!"

"Yeah," I said. "Miss Banks can dish it

out, but she can't take it."

"I guess we showed her," said Alexia. "Revenge is sweet!"

It felt great to get back at Miss Banks. But then Little Miss Wet-Blanket had to chime in.

"But wait . . . What are we going to do now?" asked Andrea. "We don't have a

teacher. They're going to have to hire a new teacher."

Hmmm, no teacher. Ryan, Michael, and I snapped into action and did what we always do when there's no grown-up in the room. We got up on our desks and shook our butts at the class. It was hilarious.

And you'll never believe who walked through the door at that moment.

Nobody! How many times do I have to tell you? PEOPLE CAN'T WALK THROUGH DOORS! You should really pay more attention when you're reading. But you'll never believe who walked through the door*way*.

It was Miss Banks!

"Eeeeeek!" screamed Alexia. "She's back!"

"As I was saying," Miss Banks told us, "starting tomorrow, we're going to work on natural resources and ecosystems and—"

"Wait a minute," I interrupted her. "You said that you quit."

"Yeah!" everybody agreed.

"Quit?" said Miss Banks with a laugh. "Don't be silly. I was just pranking you! You're stuck with me for the rest of the year!"

"NOOOOOOOOOOOOOOOOOOOOOOO!"

Well, that's pretty much what happened. Maybe Miss Banks will stop pulling pranks on us all the time. Maybe I'll get some *real* brownies, doughnuts, gum, and Oreos that aren't filled with tooth-paste. Maybe a truck full of quadrilaterals will fall on Andrea's head. Maybe I'll learn how to spell "splurgle" and "spinkheimer." Maybe I'll run away to Antarctica and go live with the penguins. Maybe an aster-oid will strike the earth tonight so I won't have to go back to fourth grade. Maybe somebody will invent a voice-activated paper towel dispenser. Maybe we'll find a Sloop Lirpa.

But it won't be easy!

NOTE TO READERS

At the end of *My Weirder-est School #12*, it said there was a mistake in the book and it would be explained in *My Weirdtastic School #1*. Well, here it is: when the kids finally opened their math books to page 23, it said $2 + 2 = 4$. But actually, back in *My Weirder School #7* it was already revealed what was on page 23—the eleven times table.

Special thanks to my Facebook followers, who gave me many of the ideas for the pranks in this book: James Hawkins, Jakob Nedlberg, Kelly LaCombe Brusgard, Sandra Lynn Macias, Jason Carr, Nina Maria, Tracey Jarossy, Laura Slattery Wiggins, Juli Gordon Olson, Heidi Margaret, Lise Criswell, Linda Davino

Piro, Anne Adamakos DeDona, Melissa Millintschuk Lewert, Jackie Lugg, Tiffany Ryals, Julie Ruminer, Melanie Beth, Suzanne Flick Kurasz, and Kristin Cerbone.

More weird books from Dan Gutman

My Weird School

My Weird School Graphic Novels

My Weirder School

My Weirdest School

My Weirder-est School

My Weird School Fast Facts

My Weird School Daze

My Weird Tips